Iktomi
and the
Berries

Orchard Books   New York

Also by Paul Goble:
Iktomi and the Boulder

I don't like it—
That white guy, Paul Goble,
is telling stories
about me again....

Iktomi
and the
Berries

a Plains Indian story

retold and illustrated
by PAUL GOBLE

for Janet, with all my love

References

Ella Deloria, *Dakota Texts*, Publications of the American Ethnological Society, Vol. 14, New York, 1932; Richard Erdoes, *The Sound of Flutes*, Pantheon Books, New York, 1976; George Bird Grinnell, *By Cheyenne Campfires*, Yale University Press, New Haven, 1926; Walter McClintock, *The Old North Trail*, Macmillan, London, 1910; Sally Old Coyote and Joy Yellowtail Toineeta, *Indian Tales of the Northern Plains*, Montana Reading Publications, Billings, 1972; R. D. Theisz, ed., *Buckskin Tokens*, North Plains Press, Aberdeen, 1975; Clark Wissler and David J. Duvall, *Mythology of the Blackfoot Indians*, Anthropological Papers of the American Museum of Natural History, Vol. 2, New York, 1909.

Orchard Books, 95 Madison Avenue, New York, NY 10016. Manufactured in the United States of America. Book design by Paul Goble. The text of this book is set in 22 pt. Zapf Book Light. The illustrations are India ink and watercolor reproduced in combined line and halftone. Library of Congress Cataloging-in-Publication Data. Goble, Paul. Iktomi and the berries / Paul Goble, p. cm. "A Richard Jackson book" — Half title p. Summary: Relates Iktomi's fruitless efforts to pick some buffalo berries. ISBN 0-531-05819-0 (tr.)   ISBN 0-531-08419-1 (lib. bdg.) ISBN 0-531-07029-8 (pbk.) 1. Indians of North America—Great Plains—Legends. [1. Indians of North America—Great Plains—Legends.] I. Title. E78.G73G62 1989 398.2'08997—dc19 [E] 88-23353
10 9 8 7 6 5 4 3 2

About Iktomi

Native Americans tell many amusing stories about their trickster. They call him by different names. Iktomi (*eek-toe-me*), his Lakota (Sioux) name, means spider. He is a man who, like the spider of folk literature, is very clever, but also very stupid. He gets into things that are not his business; he tricks people and is tricked himself; and he is always showing off. Everyone enjoys hearing about Iktomi's disreputable ways, and certainly without meaning to, he gives us the precious gift of laughter!

In Lakota Creation stories, Iktomi sometimes uses his cleverness to benefit man, rather than for mischief. For example, people say that the shape of the cottonwood leaf gave Iktomi the idea to make the first tipis and moccasins. The white man, with his wonderful and useful inventions, and also his untrustworthiness, seems to the Cheyennes to embody the same conflicting characteristics, and they use *Veho*, their word for the spider trickster, to mean white man, as well.

Children learn what is unacceptable from Iktomi's terrible behavior, without the need for moralizing. The words of the stories are colloquial because Iktomi has no respect for the finer points of language. Each storyteller weaves a story around familiar themes. Iktomi is still alive today, and people speak of him in the present tense: "He is like some tourists who come into an Indian village not knowing how to behave or what to do, trying to impress everybody," (Raechel Strange Owl). "He's a foolish guy, a smart ass…." (Lame Deer).

The stories are told mostly at night when children are ready for sleep. Grown-ups listen too, and the storyteller expects a certain amount of good-natured prompting. Children have to say "*han, han,*" (a nasal "harn") from time to time to let the storyteller know they are listening. When there are no more "*hans,*" it is assumed that they must be asleep….

A Note for the Reader

Where the text changes to italic, readers may wish to give their listeners a chance to make their own remarks about Iktomi. These stories are always told with comments interjected by the storyteller and the listeners about the stupidity of believing anything Iktomi says or does. Iktomi's additional thoughts, printed in small type, need not be read aloud, but may be mentioned when showing the pictures.

Iktomi was walking along....
Every story about Iktomi
starts the same way.

Iktomi was walking along.
The sun had just risen,
and he was out hunting.

Today I'm going hunting
in the old traditional way.

My wig

My quiver of arrows

Coil of rope for tying
up meat

My strike-a-light bag

My skinning knife

My ash-wood bow

My coyote skin disguise

Do I look all right?
I'm not over-dressed, am I?

"I'll shoot some prairie dogs and give
all my friends and relatives a feast,"
he said to himself.
"That will impress them!
'Ikto,' they'll say, 'you're a great hunter.
You're *so* generous; we love you.'"
Iktomi thinks a lot of himself.
He is forever boasting about
something he is going to do.

Do you think anyone would ever want
to eat prairie dog?

Iktomi was wearing a coyote skin
over his head.
"When I put this on," he said,
"the birds and animals think I'm
just another old coyote."
He doesn't look much like one, does he?
"My ancestors lived for thousands and
thousands of years by hunting.
I've got hunting in my blood."

Yes, my ancestors knew a
thing or two about hunting—
so do I.

How's that, Robin Hood?

It's getting hot under here.

By this time, the sun was overhead,
and Iktomi was still walking.
"There aren't any prairie dogs nowadays,"
he told himself. "The white people
killed all the buffaloes.
Now they haven't left me
a single prairie dog."

*Do you think he can see anything
under that coyote skin?*

I'm a great hunter.
Watch me.

Iktomi stalked stealthily about,
with an arrow ready against his bowstring.
He looked this way…
and that way.

*He never noticed that all the
prairie dogs were laughing at him!*

Iktomi was hot, thirsty, and very hungry.
His insides rumbled and grumbled at him:
"Ikto, you really must give us
something to eat," they growled.
"Be quiet," Iktomi replied to his stomach.
"How can I hunt if you make
all that noise?
Can't you *see* that you're frightening
all the birds and animals away?"

Why didn't I wait for
my wife to cook my
breakfast?

"No. This isn't any good," Iktomi thought.
"It's always the same:
Just when you really want something
you can never find it.
I'll go to the river
and shoot some ducks instead."

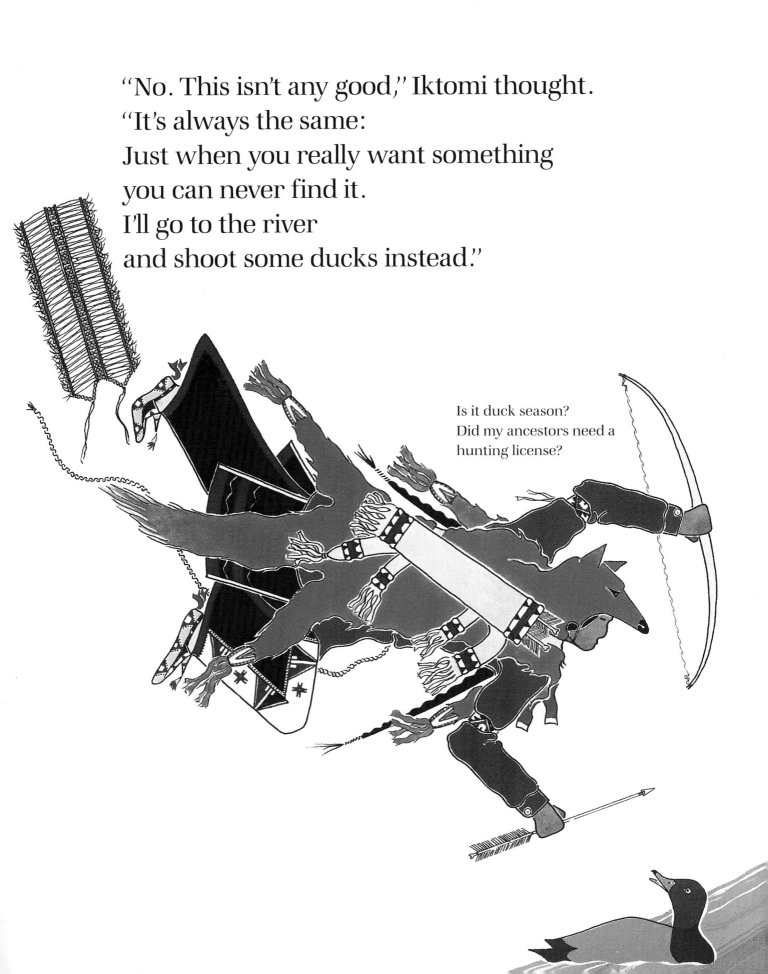

Is it duck season?
Did my ancestors need a
hunting license?

Iktomi crawled cautiously
toward the river.
Closer and closer he came.
He could hear the ducks talking.

*Do you think they, too, are watching him
and laughing?*

What happened?
Who pushed me?

Iktomi never saw that the bank
overhung the river.
It broke under him and he fell in
head first with a terrific splash.

All the ducks flew away.

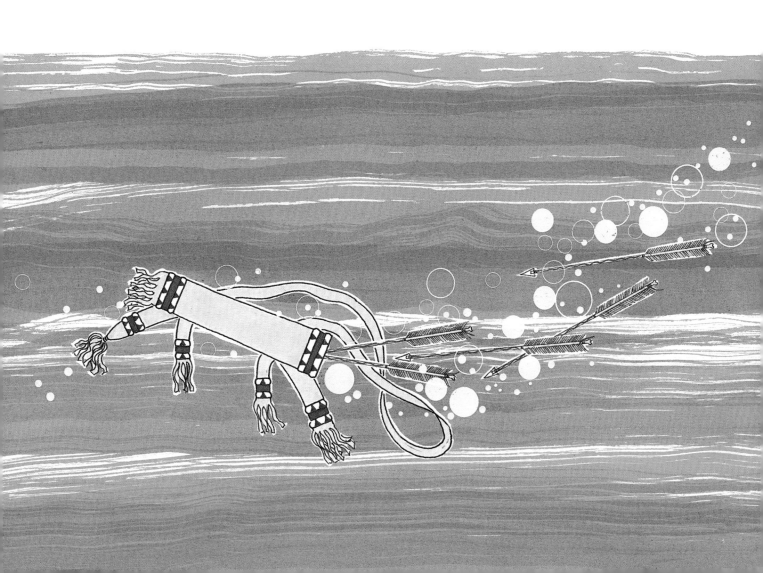

Dripping wet, he sat beside the river.
Iktomi was totally disgusted.
"I'm so hungry...."

Just then he spotted some beautiful
red berries in the water.
"Ah! Fresh fruit! That's better!
That's exactly what I've been looking
for all morning!"

Is that true?

"I'll make berry soup.
My relatives will like that best of all.
'Ikto,' they'll say,
'we just l-o-v-e your berry soup.
We must have your recipe.'
I'll get some ducks tomorrow."

Do you think so?

Imagine berries
growing in the water....
Oh, the wonders of nature!

Where am I?

"Ha!" cried Iktomi. "Berries
can't get away from me."
And with that he jumped into the river.

He felt around in the water.
"Where are they?" he asked.
"I should have taken off this coyote skin;
I can't see anything."

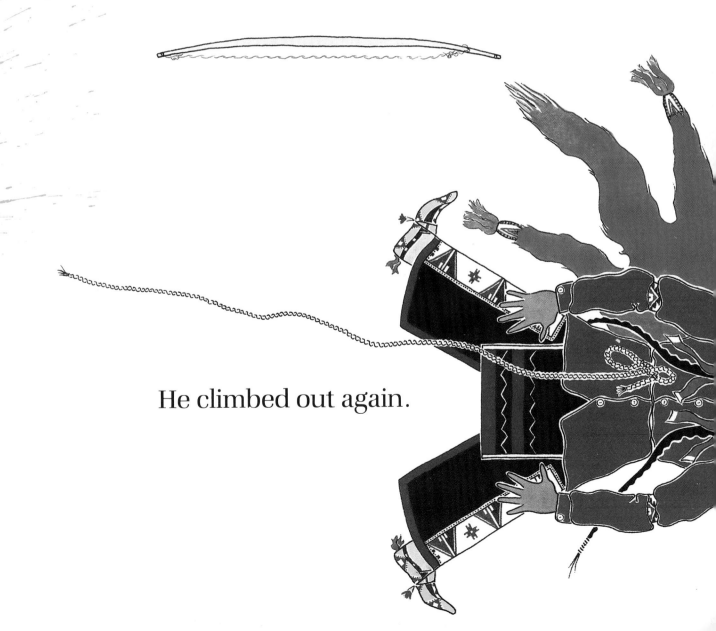

He climbed out again.

Iktomi looked down into the water.
"Yes! There they are."
He jumped in again
and felt all around....
No berries....
"I must have the wrong place,"
he sighed, as he climbed
back onto the bank.

Just watch this fancy dive!

"No! There they are sure enough.
How silly of me not to have seen them.
Third time lucky! Here goes!"
Iktomi dived straight down to the bottom—
and got his mouth full of mud.

Do you think he even knows how to swim?

"Everything is going against
me today," he complained.

Where are they?
They were here a moment ago.

"If I could just stay down
there longer I would be sure
to find those berries."

"I've got an idea. Yes! That's it!"
Iktomi took his coil of rope,
and tied one end around his neck.
He tied the other end around
the largest rock he could lift.
"This is a heavy rock.
This will keep me down there longer,"
he thought to himself.

Hey! Don't be so rough.

"Those berries won't get away
from me now."
Don't you think that was a stupid idea?

Iktomi took a deep breath—
swung the rock:
"One…*two*…*THREE*…" into the water—
and was jerked off the bank after it.

The rock sank down,
down,
dragging Iktomi
to the bottom of the river.

"This is better,"
he thought to himself.
"Now I'm right at the bottom."
He searched in every direction,
but he still couldn't find any berries.

Iktomi groped around on the riverbed
until he just had to come up for air.
But he had forgotten the rock
tied around his neck....

He tried lifting it, but he couldn't
swim with such a heavy weight.
"Rock, let go of me!"
He fumbled with the knot in utter panic....
"Oh HELP!!"

Down we go!

It certainly looks like the end of Ikto.

Oh, poor Ikto....
What a way to die!
What *will* people think?

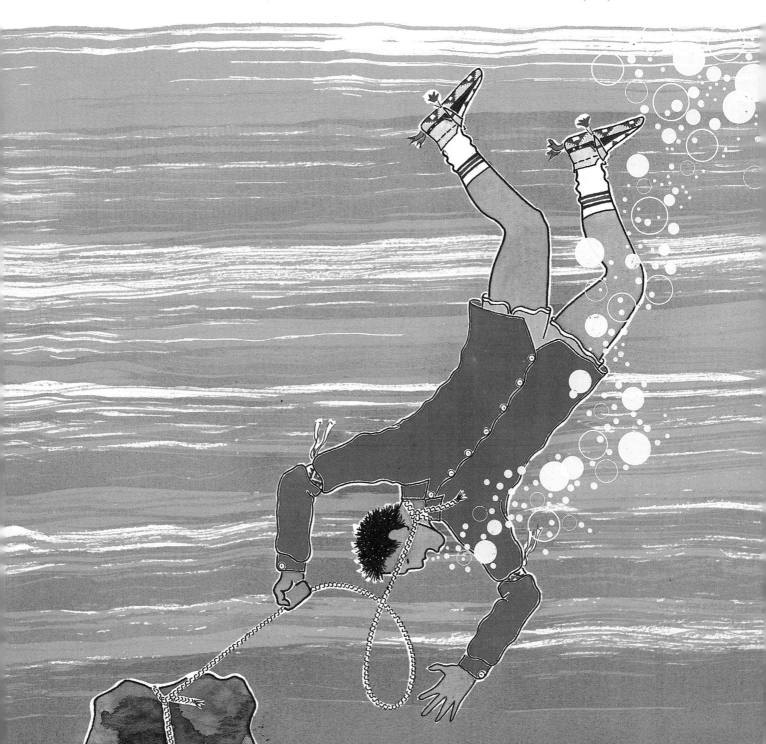

Do you think it is?

Where's my wig?
I've lost my leggings.

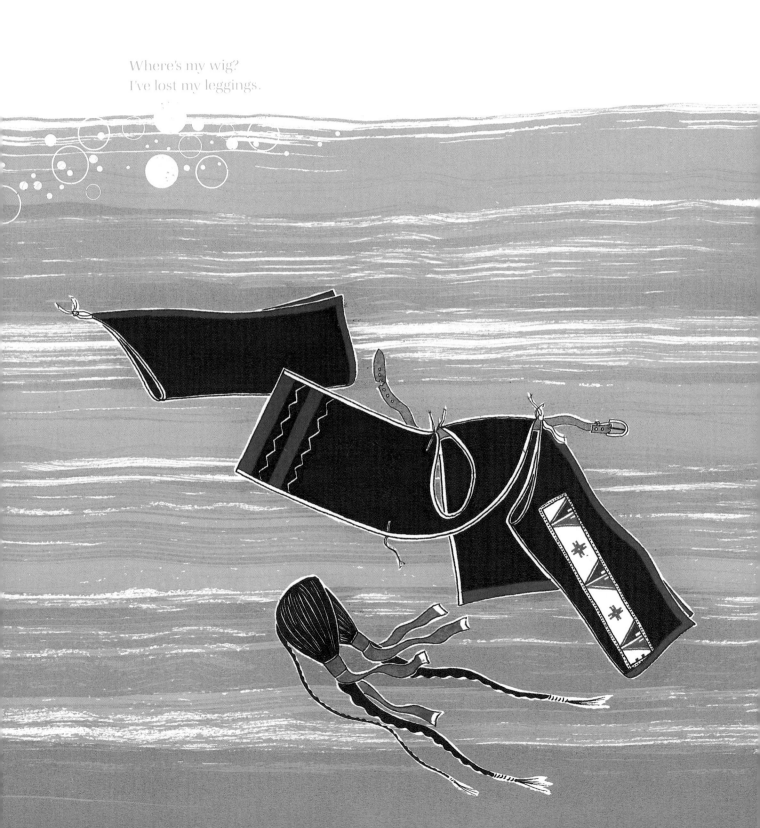

He was full of water and just about dead
when he floated to the surface again.
He crawled onto the bank,
gasping for air....
"I should have stayed in bed
this morning," he decided.

Exhausted, he turned and lay on his back.

"That's odd..." he thought.
He was looking up at the berries
in the bushes above his head!
All the while he had been seeing
their reflection in the water....
"Oh no! I hope nobody saw me."

How did those berries
get up there?

Anyway, I bet those
berries were sour.

Iktomi snatched up his bow
and set about beating the bushes.
He lost his temper completely
and lashed at them right and left.
"Take that!—and *that*!—and *THAT*!
you brainless berry bushes.
Don't you ever dare to try and
trick me like that again!
DO YOU HEAR ME?
From now on everyone will beat you
when they pick your berries."

Iktomi was so angry that he never
stopped until he had knocked
all the berries off the branches.
They floated off down the river,
and the ducks had a fine feast.

That was a day which Iktomi
does not wish to remember.

Iktomi went on his way again….

*Does anyone know what
Iktomi will get up to next?*

Let me think:
What was I going to do?
Oh yes, I'm hungry.
I'll get a hamburger.
Nothing to drink….

*People pick buffalo berries after
the first frosts of fall.
They spread cloths under the bushes
and beat the branches with sticks,
just like Iktomi did.*